The Big Fib

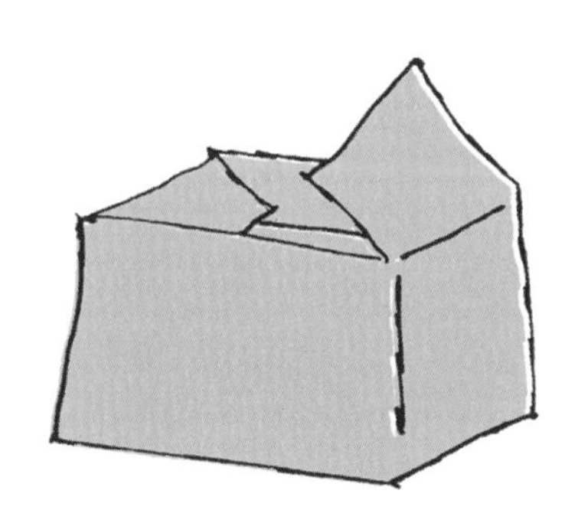

I Like to Read® books, created by award-winning picture book artists as well as talented newcomers, instill confidence and the joy of reading in new readers.

We want to hear every new reader say, "I like to read!"

Visit our website for flash cards and activities:
www.holidayhouse.com/ILiketoRead
#ILTR

This book has been tested by an educational expert and determined to be a guided reading level E.

The Big Fib

by Tim Hamilton

I Like to Read®

HOLIDAY HOUSE • NEW YORK

Printed and Bound in November 2017 at Tien Wah Press, Johor Bahru, Johor, Malaysia.
The artwork was created with pen and ink,
watercolors, and digital tools.
www.holidayhouse.com
5 7 9 10 8 6 4

Library of Congress Cataloging-in-Publication Data
Hamilton, Tim.
The big fib / by Tim Hamilton. — First edition.
pages cm. — (I like to read)
Summary: After playing with Miss Finn's discarded boxes and
making a mess, her young neighbors first lie about their misdeed
and then make things right.
ISBN 978-0-8234-2939-4 (hardcover)
[1. Honesty—Fiction. 2. Behavior—Fiction. 3. Boxes—Fiction.
4. Imagination—Fiction.]
I. Title.
PZ7.H1826588Big 2014
[E]—dc23
2013009705

ISBN 978-0-8234-3312-4 (paperback)

For my wife, Jean,
who knows that the truth
is mightier than the fib

One day
Miss Finn got rid of
a lot of boxes.

We took some boxes
and made a train.

Then we played a train game.
We went far, far, far.

We took two more boxes
and made race cars.

Then we played
a race car game.
We went fast, fast, fast.

We took more
and made a jet.

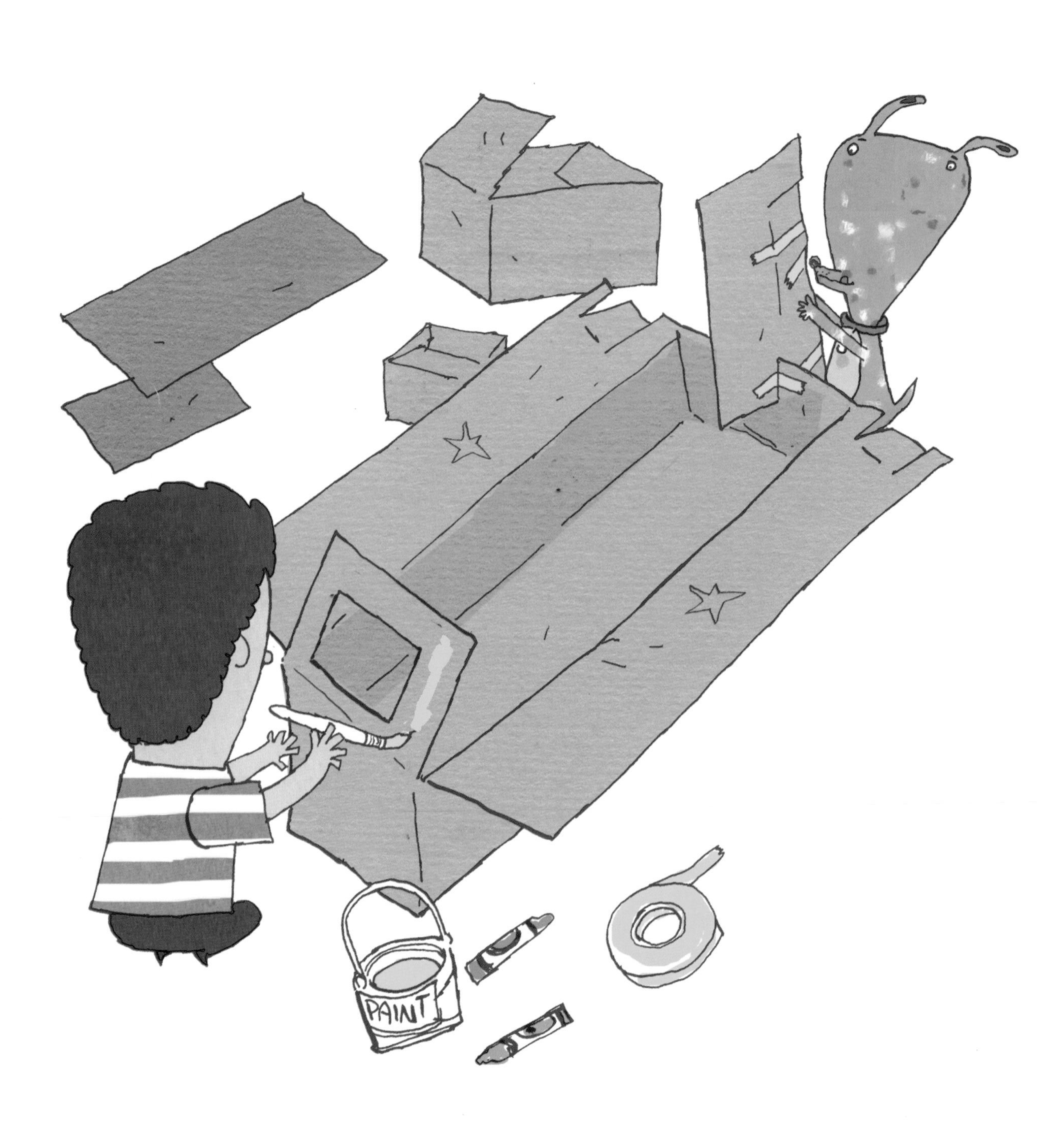

We went up, up, up.

Miss Finn came out.
"Who made this mess?"
she said.

"The wind,"
I said.
But that was
a big fib.

“The wind?” said Miss Finn.
My big fib got bigger.
“It was a big wind,” I said.

Miss Finn picked up the boxes.

She was slow,
slow, slow.

"We will pick up the boxes,"
I said. "The wind didn't
make the mess.
We did."

"I'm glad you told the truth,"
said Miss Finn.
Then she gave us milk
and cookies.

“Let’s play a game,”
said Miss Finn.
“I am queen.
You are my knights.
And we are friends.”

"You don't have to play
that we are friends,"
I said. "That is real."

You will like these too!

Dinosaurs Don't, Dinosaurs Do
by Steve Björkman

Fish Had a Wish by Michael Garland
Kirkus Reviews Best Children's Books list
and Top 25 Children's Books list

I Said, "Bed!" by Bruce Degen

I Will Try by Marilyn Janovitz

Look! by Ted Lewin

Pete Won't Eat by Emily Arnold McCully

See Me Run by Paul Meisel
A Theodor Seuss Geisel Award Honor Book

See more I Like to Read books.
Go to www.holidayhouse.com/I-Like-to-Read.

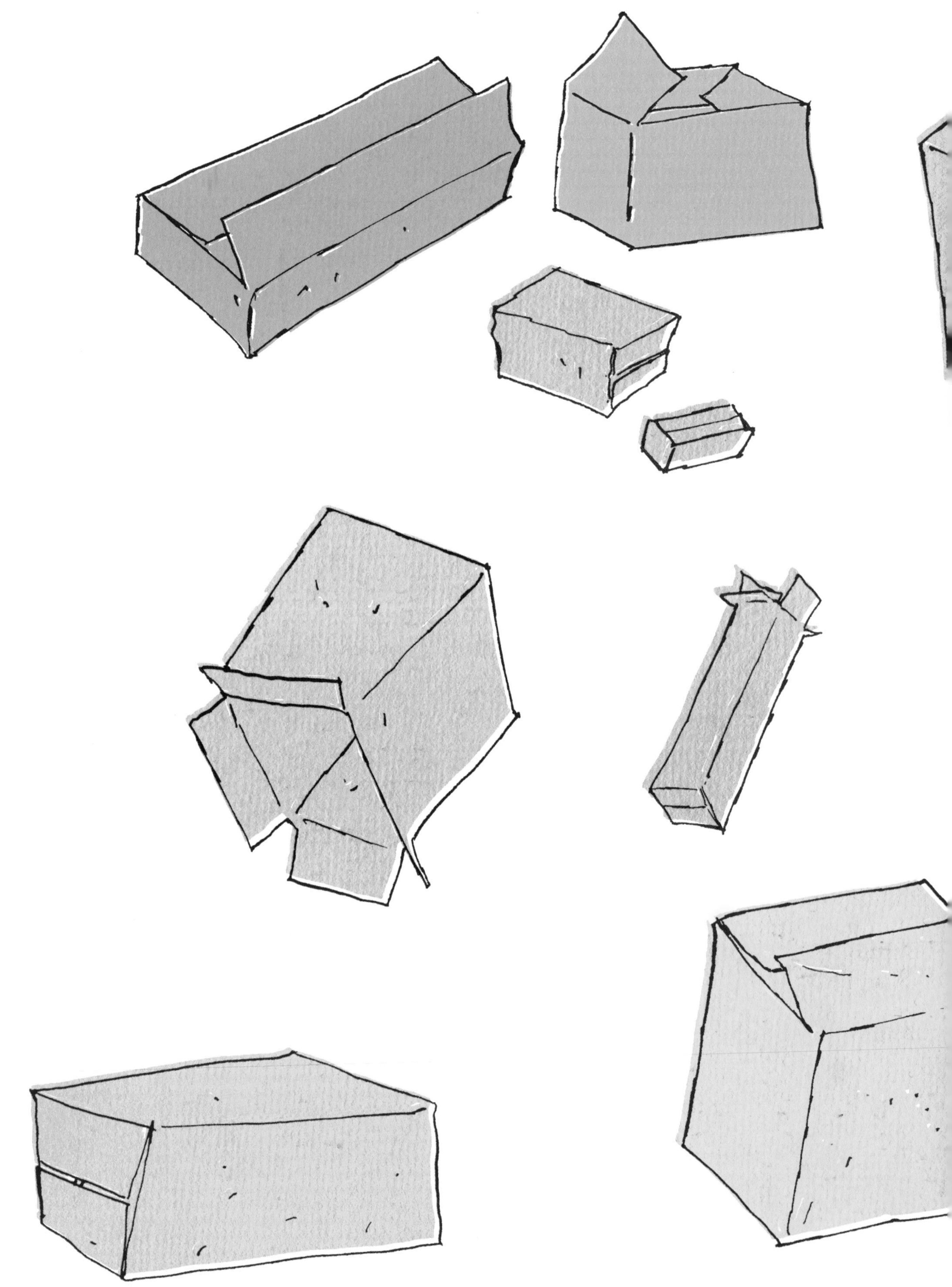

I Like to Read® Books in Paperback
You will like all of them!

Bad Dog by David McPhail
The Big Fib by Tim Hamilton
Boy, Bird, and Dog by David McPhail
Can You See Me? by Ted Lewin
Car Goes Far by Michael Garland
Come Back, Ben by Ann Hassett and John Hassett
The Cowboy by Hildegard Müller
Dinosaurs Don't, Dinosaurs Do by Steve Björkman
Ed and Kip by Kay Chorao
The End of the Rainbow by Liza Donnelly
Fireman Fred by Lynn Rowe Reed
Fish Had a Wish by Michael Garland
The Fly Flew In by David Catrow
Good Night, Knight by Betsy Lewin
Grace by Kate Parkinson
Happy Cat by Steve Henry
I Have a Garden by Bob Barner
I Said, "Bed!" by Bruce Degen
I Will Try by Marilyn Janovitz
Late Nate in a Race by Emily Arnold McCully
The Lion and the Mice by Rebecca Emberley and Ed Emberley
Little Ducks Go by Emily Arnold McCully
Look! by Ted Lewin
Look Out, Mouse! by Steve Björkman
Me Too! by Valeri Gorbachev
Mice on Ice by Rebecca Emberley and Ed Emberley
Pete Won't Eat by Emily Arnold McCully
Pig Has a Plan by Ethan Long
Ping Wants to Play by Adam Gudeon
Sam and the Big Kids by Emily Arnold McCully
See Me Dig by Paul Meisel
See Me Run by Paul Meisel
A THEODOR SEUSS GEISEL AWARD HONOR BOOK
Sick Day by David McPhail
3, 2, 1, Go! by Emily Arnold McCully
What Am I? Where Am I? by Ted Lewin
You Can Do It! by Betsy Lewin

Visit http://www.holidayhouse.com/I-Like-to-Read/ for more about I Like to Read® books, including flash cards, reproducibles, and the complete list of titles.